THIS WALKER BOOK BELONGS TO:

_____

_____

_____

_____

To Alison, with much love
Viv

For Martha and Sophie, with love
Chris

First published 1994 by
Walker Books Ltd, 87 Vauxhall Walk
London SE11 5HJ

This edition published 1995

2 4 6 8 10 9 7 5 3 1

Text © 1994 Vivian French
Illustrations © 1994 Chris Fisher

This book was typeset in Perpetua.

Printed in Hong Kong

British Library Cataloguing in Publication Data
A catalogue record for this book is
available from the British Library.

ISBN 0-7445-4315-0

PRINCESS PRIMROSE

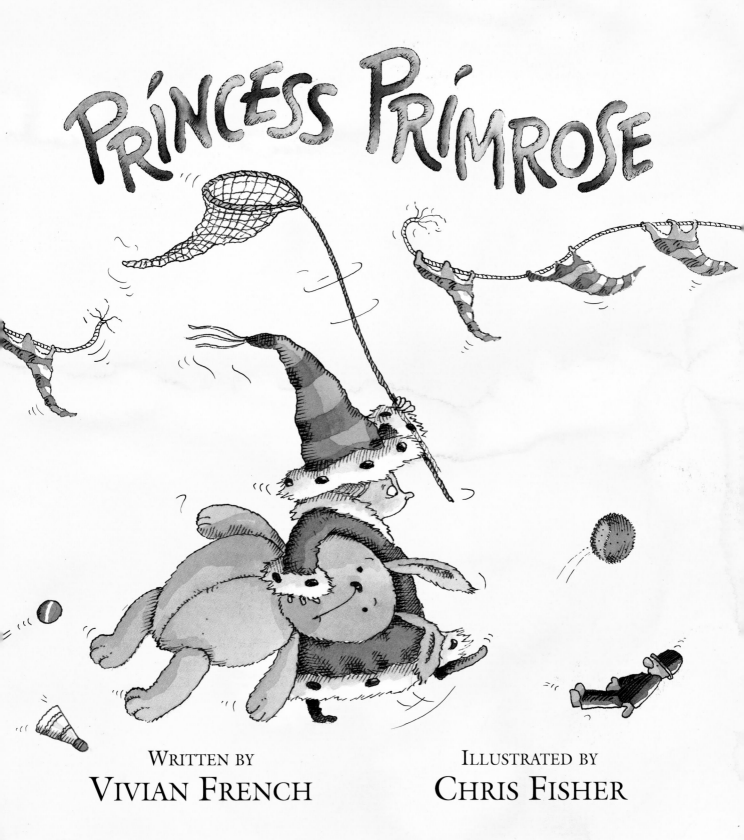

WRITTEN BY
VIVIAN FRENCH

ILLUSTRATED BY
CHRIS FISHER

WALKER BOOKS
AND SUBSIDIARIES
LONDON • BOSTON • SYDNEY

PRINCESS PRIMROSE
woke up early
on her birthday
and marched downstairs.

"Where are my presents?" she demanded as she sat down at the breakfast table.

"Shut your eyes, my tiddly umpty birthday poppet," said the Queen.

"No peeping!" said the King. The Cook came in with a pile of presents.

The Cook's boy came behind her, carrying the teapot.

"NOW!" they all said.
Princess Primrose
opened her eyes.
"Happy birthday,
my darling sweetest
pudding," said the Queen.
"Oh," said Primrose,
and she tore the paper
off her presents.

"A teddy bear
and a train set. HUH!
I wanted a gold coach
with six white horses."

"Happy birthday,
my itsy bitsy princess,"
said the King.
"What's this?" said
Primrose, ripping
open another parcel.
"BAH! A skipping rope.
I wanted my very own
magician with a blue cloak
with silver stars on it."

"Happy birthday,
Princess Primrose,"
said the Cook.
"YUCK!" said Primrose.
"A cookery book. I
wanted a magic mirror."

The Cook's boy stared at Primrose.
"Isn't she rude?" he whispered.
"Sssh, dear," said the Cook.

"Where's my cake?"
demanded Primrose.
"I want to blow
out my candles."

"Birthday tea at four
o'clock, my teeny
angel pussycat,"
said the Queen.

"HUMPH!"
said Primrose.
"So what are we
going to do all day?"

"Er..."
said the Queen.
"Ar..."
said the King.
"I'm just off to make
the cake," said the
Cook, and she
hurried out.

The Cook's boy tugged at the
Queen's arm. "Why don't we
play a game?"
Primrose sat up. "What did
you say?"

"Why don't we play a game?"
said the Cook's boy. "What
about hide-and-seek?"
"I don't know how," said
Primrose.

"I'll show you,"
said the Cook's boy.
"You can hide,
and I'll find you."

The Cook's boy
shut his eyes and
counted to ten while
the King and the Queen
and Primrose hid
in the attic.
"Coming! Ready
or not!" shouted
the Cook's boy.

The King shut his eyes
and counted to ten while
the Queen and Primrose
and the Cook's boy
hid in the bedroom.
"Whoopee! Here I come!"
shouted the King.

The Queen shut her
eyes and counted to ten
while Primrose and the
Cook's boy and the King
hid in the bathroom.
"Coooeee!
I'm on my way!"
called the Queen.

Primrose shut her eyes and counted to ten while the Cook's boy and the King and the Queen hid in the kitchen.

"One two three – it's ME!" she shouted, and she found the Cook's boy and the King and the Queen in no time at all.

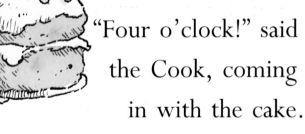

"Four o'clock!" said
the Cook, coming
in with the cake.
"Time for a lovely tea for my
bestest poppety
parcel," said
the Queen,
puffing hard.
"Bother," said
Primrose. "I want
to go on playing."
She looked at
the Cook's boy.
"You can play with
me after tea," she said.
"And tomorrow. And
the next day."
"No," said the
Cook's boy.
"I don't want to.
Well – not unless you ask nicely."

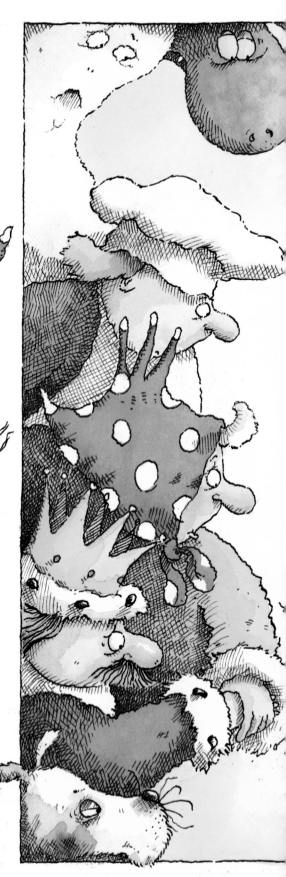

The King and the Queen and the
Cook stared at him. Then they looked
at Primrose and held their breath.
Princess Primrose made a strange
noise. The King and the Queen held
hands tightly. The noise grew louder,
and the Cook edged nearer to the door.

"P... P...

PLEASE!"

"P...P...P...PLEASE!"
said Princess Primrose.
"PLEASE will you
play with me?"

The Cook's boy bowed.
"Of course, Princess,"
he said. "It'll be fun."

P. . .

"Can we play too?" asked
the King and the Queen.
Primrose put her head on
one side. "Maybe," she said.
"If you ask nicely."

"Oh," said the King and
the Queen. "Please?"
Princess Primrose curtsied.
"Of course," she said. "And
now I want you all to sing
Happy Birthday to me."

"Well…" said the Cook's boy.
"PLEASE!" said Princess Primrose.

"It'll be a pleasure," said the Cook's boy and the
Cook and the Queen and the King. And they did.

MORE WALKER PAPERBACKS
For You to Enjoy

Also by Vivian French

ONCE UPON A TIME

illustrated by John Prater

A little boy tells of his "dull" day, while all around a
host of favourite nursery characters act out their stories.

"The pictures are excellent, the telegraphic text perfect, the idea brilliant.
We have here a classic, I'm sure, with an author-reader bond
as strong as *Rosie's Walk." Books for Keeps*

0-7445-3690-1   £4.99

TOTTIE PIG'S SPECIAL BIRTHDAY

illustrated by Clive Scruton

When Tottie learns that the new baby may arrive on her birthday,
she is not pleased. But what can she do about it?

"Perfect for toddlers who are about to acquire a little brother or sister...
Tottie is a charming character and one with whom children
will immediately identify." *Tony Bradman, Parents*

0-7445-3050-4   £3.99

TOTTIE PIG'S NOISY CHRISTMAS

illustrated by Clive Scruton

Christmas in the Pig household is not as peaceful as it might be
when Tottie and her baby brother Parker get the wrong presents!

"The agony and ecstasy of Christmas is brilliantly portrayed
... a comic masterpiece of characterisation, pace and dialogue." *The Sunday Telegraph*

0-7445-2354-0   £3.99